Five Deadly Duels

By

Elcid

©2024 by Narcisse Sadi. All rights reserved. No part of this book may be reproduced in any form or by any means, electronic or mechanical, including photocopying, recording, or by any information storage and retrieval system, without permission in writing from the author.

For more info:

Official Instagram: @mackadelcid

I thank my family, friends and everything else that inspires me to write.

CHAPTER ONE- THE SERPENT HOUSE

Once upon a time, a boy of the age of seven found himself facing another boy of the same age. Both came from the same clan and, as part of their arduous training since the age of two, the two boys were to engage each other in a duel. They both stared at each other fixed and focused.

Not related by blood, but a trait shared by many in the clan was the small yellow wolf-like eyes both boys had, with epicanthic folds. One was slightly taller and chubbier, and the other skinny and shorter.

The chubbier boy charged forth screaming with a menacing facial expression, and the skinny boy did not budge, standing still. Once the chubbier boy was close enough and had launched his attack, the skinny boy, like a slithering snake, evaded the attack and then countered like a cobra seizing its prey. He struck the chubby boy from the side, hitting him in the eye with his fingers, as his hand was positioned like the head of a snake. The motion was like a snake that coils in and then out.

The chubby boy covered his face as he hopped up and down, yelling in pain, and the skinny boy, seeing more opportunities, moved in. However, he was also struck with a sudden punch to the chest that made him hit the ground as he landed on his back, with the air depleting from his lungs.

Shocked and gasping for air, he looked up and saw a man standing beside him, the assailant whose punch had knocked him down. The man looked at him sternly, as if he had failed. "Do not be too eager and always observe your surroundings!" barked the man. The man then turned to the chubbier boy who had stopped yelling in pain and was now covering his one swollen eye. He strolled towards him calmly, and in an instant, a slap from his hand brushed the chubbier boy's face, knocking him straight down. "Size and stupid intimidations are signs of fear!" bellowed the man. He then turned to the skinnier boy and grunted, "Get up, Silver!" and to the chubby boy, "You too, Medillo!"

Both boys quickly got up to their feet, with Medillo still covering his eye, and a quick glare from the man suddenly made him uncover his eye, which remained shut. The man was their instructor and Silver's uncle, Snakequill, ruthless and a disciplinarian. He trained the boys in the ways of the Slang Nyoka clan. The Slang Nyoka was a clan of assassins used by nations, groups, or the likes to carry out assassinations. Living in deep secrecy, the clan had positioned itself on the outskirts of the Dragons' Lair, not far from a nearby forest enclosing a large mountain, which was home to variously connected caves, another area where the clan dwelled.

The basis of the training of the clan was in its secret heritage of the "Serpent Style," the clan's secret martial art. The father of the Snake Style, which was practised in the South, in the Loham Temple. The monks there had been taught bits of the Serpent style by a renegade member of the Slang Nyoka clan. And they had to formulate their own version because still adhering to the clan's secret ways, this renegade member who had ventured hundreds of years ago to the temple never completely taught the whole martial art.

Silver Serpent was a member of the ruling Serpent House, which had founded the clan under Kobak Serpent, the founding patriarch of the clan and the Serpent House itself. The current High Priest was Silver's father, Quicksand Silver, and his wife, Silver's mother, served as the Queen Mother, and her name was Halina Silver. Silver was the firstborn and had three younger siblings, one that was five years old, the other was four years old, and the last was two years old and was his youngest sister, Helga. The other two were boys, the one that was five years old was Jin and the one that was four years old was Quiller.

Being the eldest son, Silver was something of a prodigy, and regardless of his innate talent, he trained as if he had no skill. Day and night, he trained with his rival and training brother, Medillo, who was from an affluent family of the clan, whose father was amongst the counseling elders who counseled the Grand Priest in the daily matters of the clan. With the coming years and the changes in the world with the added influence of Snakequill, the clan began falling into chaos.

During a banquet, a time when the clan took it easy and celebrated, the Grand Priest was poisoned by none other than his brother Snakequill. Halina, the queen mother, was stabbed to death, and a shocked Silver witnessed all this amid the chaos. It was quick and horrific. He was only eighteen years old at the time and had just come back from a mission with Medillo, where they had assassinated the heads of a crime group from Feiville.

Prior to the banquet, Silver had confessed to Medillo that he had no interest in remaining in the clan or being the next heir to the throne. Instead, Silver mentioned he wanted to test his skills as a martial artist by traveling and dueling. Silver was inspired by the stories of Daruma Chan, an ancient warrior who had left his home in the Sol Islands, venturing off in an odyssey of martial exchange. However, being of the Slang Nyoka, Silver's dream was to duel to the death and reach the high number of five hundred duels. "Five hundred, that is my number and then I can legitimately say I am of ability," he said before Medillo shook his head and sniggered.

Having discovered the murderer and creator of the discord was his uncle, Silver was more motivated to leave. He was not interested in the politics and taking the reins, to Medillo's disgust, and the two got into a scuffle after a heated argument in a cold night in the surrounding forest, outside the Slang Nyoka's cave dwelling. Only the full moon's dim light shed them some light.

"YOU TRAITOR! SCUM!" bellowed a furious Medillo, now also eighteen years of age and no longer chubby but very muscular and tall like a moving mountain. Silver had turned his back to walk away, and Medillo grabbed him by slapping the back of his head. A shaking tremor shivered all the way down to his feet as Medillo then yanked him back, sending him flying against a tree.

Getting up and infuriated, Silver's eyes widened, and for the first time, he exposed Medillo to what he was capable of. Medillo suddenly began to feel the air thinning with each breath, and a frown immediately painted itself on his face. He felt himself slightly choking, he glared at Silver and charged for him. Silver then grinned in evil delight as Medillo, with the sudden movements, suddenly felt a great depletion in energy. Struggling to breathe, he stopped and fought hard, resisting, and things got worse. His vision blurred, and then everything became dark for a sudden that when he opened his eyes, it was the next day. His eyes met a sun that glared, and he blinked quickly getting up as he glanced around with no sight of Silver. Medillo

had a wry smile appear on his face as he muttered, "Cheeky bastard."

CHAPTER TWO- LOVE AND MURDER

The man whom Silver had punched was making choking noises that caught Katya's attention as she glanced anxiously at him, but her head was turned back by Silver as he gently turned her head back to him. 'Let's go,' he muttered. Resisting a bit, she asked, 'Are you sure that he is alright?' Silver, remaining silent, grabbed her hand again, and they began to walk. Then he said as he turned to her, 'Your troubles are gone, do not worry about the rest.'

Walking, they remained close and connected as they held each other's hands and headed towards the venue where the brawls were taking place. 'I have a question... what are you doing in such a seedy place?' Silver asked, and Katya smirked before replying as she let go of his hand. He stared at her up and down, ending back at her lips, mesmerized by her beauty. He did not understand the intrigue or the hole he was falling in. 'I am just a girl trying to have fun,' she eventually said. The answer disturbed Silver, and it did not make sense, but he quickly brushed this off. He was entrapped, like a fly stuck in a web; the difference, a fly would fight in vain to free itself, while Silver liked it.

By the time they had headed to the venue to watch the fights, the man outside whom Silver had punched had fallen flat on his face, his eyes staring astray. And his mouth was slightly open; the source of a pool of blood his head rested on.

He did not fight anyone that night. Instead, he stayed up erect, in a cocktail of arousal and confusion for the emotions he felt for this strange woman he had just met. Katya had told him she was twenty years old; she did not tell him anymore. And he did not bother asking her her last name, as he kept quiet about himself as well. In fact, she was intrigued by his strength and courage. He did tell her that he was a martial artist, and that was about it. She had also sensed he wanted to keep his background a secret. And before the evening had ended, she had got really close to his face; she could feel he was nervous. Silver had never spent a night with a woman; Medillo had indulged in such pleasures and sometimes teased Silver of not being a man. However, those insults never fazed him. Nevertheless, he was so overwhelmed he froze and simply grabbed her posterior as he felt himself harden. She grinned at the gesture and kissed him. He simply went with the flow, until she detached. She smiled at him muttering 'Thank you,' and then she left.

Everything that had happened that evening, he played back in his mind. Living in a bar, where he had found work as the bar cleaner and was given an empty room where he could sleep. The pay was slavery, but Silver did not mind. He knew it was not for too long. The bar was run by an obese sleazeball of an owner. Silver tolerated him, even when he put his hand on his shoulders for too long, something that made Silver feel uncomfortable. Late into the evening, the owner stormed into his room. Silver's fantasizing over Katya was disturbed by the owner's presence. The man looked drunk and his eyes were red. 'Boy… you gonna give me that butt tonight…' pausing the owner stretched his hands, and Silver, who lay on his bed, quickly got up. He may have been a virgin, but he was not naïve. He knew what the owner wanted, and there was no way he was going to put up with that. The bar owner did not know who he was dealing with and blankly staring at the owner, Silver began to hiss.

'Beautiful mouth, but I want your butt!' said the owner, and he rushed forth excited. He then received an explosive front kick from Silver, causing him to fly out of the room. He landed hard on his back and panting for air, he tilted his head up catching a glimpse of Silver who stood on top. That was the last thing he saw as Silver struck him between his eyebrows with his hand positioned like the head of a snake. The owner immediately closed his eyes, and his head tilted back down and to the side. He was dead, and this time Silver was not going to be careless, packing the little he had and leaving. The flames he had lit finally engulfed the whole bar a few minutes after he had left.

The blazing flames burning the bar were too strong, that the firemen who put down the flames knew that should anything or anyone be in the bar, they were beyond rescue. The police had later arrived, cordoning off the area from the crowd and beginning their investigative work.

It was the early hours of the morning, and Feiville was still dark in the night. A man had just finished smoking his cigarette and threw it to the ground before stepping on it with his black shiny shoes, making sure it was no longer. He then gently caressed his thick black moustache, taking off his hat and moved his hand down his oily black hair, before he put his hat back on. He was pale, with sharp light blue eyes and had a hawkish facial expression. Tired with subtle bags under his eyes, it was the caffeine coursing through his veins that kept him up at that time.

'Detective Dawson!' said a man dressed in police uniform, as he rushed to the man who had just crushed his cigarette. The man who had crushed his cigarette was Detective Dawson, and he had slightly turned his head and blankly stared at the police officer who made his way towards him. Once he was close to the detective he continued, 'We found nothing yet, besides a burned body inside the bar that is beyond recognition. However, we can make out that it must be the owner. He was known to be obese and the body or its structure is that of an obese or large man. Also, the owner is known on record to be a former child rapist and sex offender.' 'I love justice,' began Detective Dawson, 'but what the fuck am I doing here? I could be getting my dick sucked, but I am here hearing about a burned-up child rapist, we should be celebrating that such scums are no longer with us the living.' Detective Dawson then turned his back to the surprised police officer as he lit another cigarette.

A week later, a man walked to a bar and minutes later walked out with a brown paper bag, he then took a nice stroll down the road towards his car. Once by his car, he placed the key in to open the driver's door and turned his head as he sensed a presence. Leaving the key by the door, he immediately drew out this gun, as he stared at a hooded figure. The man looked shaken but held his gun steadily. 'You better back away, or I will shoot!' he snarled at the hooded man. At this point, the hooded man simply removed his hoody and was revealed by the bright street lights to be Silver. Blank and still silent he stared at the man who pointed the gun. 'What are you? Some retard! I will shoot you if you do not turn your back and back away!' this time the man took a few steps forward as he gained some courage. Then, he felt his breath get thin, he coughed and beat his chest making sure he kept an eye on Silver. But with the adrenaline he felt the air getting thinner, grabbing his throat he began feeling as if he was being choked and before he knew it, he passed out. Silver strolled towards the man and took the brown paper bag. He opened it and saw rolls of cash, the amount there would help him in finding a suitable place to stay and assist with his needs.

With the coming weeks, his name and face were known in the underground fighting scene. He had fought all his opponents to their deaths. Amassing a staggering a hundred duels, each one with him being a victor.

On the night of his hundredths victory, glimpses of a woman with red hair made his heart momentarily stop. It was Katya, he had kind of forgotten about her, however, her presence resurfaced emotions he had managed to bury.

Katya was again being harassed it seemed by a large man, and Silver ignored him as he walked towards her. She smiled once she saw and so did Silver, who then turned to the man looking at him with a glare. The man knew who Silver was and immediately back away, 'She is all yours,' he said and then walked away.

'You have become quite the champion I see,' said Katya. Silver simply smiled, 'None of these brawlers are true martial artists and these fights have been too easy...I need a real challenge,' he said. 'Geez... I think someone needs to humbled,' said Katya as she placed her finger on Silver's chest. He looked shocked at first and stopped his defensive mechanism from kicking in, as he thought of multiple ways of breaking her hand and arm. Her vulnerability also turned him on as he then stared at her and she did back. Not thinking next, Silver allowed Katya to place her whole hand on his chest and then suddenly pulled her in and she slightly groaned. Then their lips touched, and they kissed before Katya pulled away and muttered, 'Let's get out of here.'

Silver then took her to an Inn where he now rented a room. They had resumed their kissing, this laying on the bed with Silver on top. He then began to hump her, unable to help himself and that is when Katya pulled away moving her hands up, so Silver could get off. And he immediately did so as he looked back at her confused. 'Sorry,' she said, 'I really like you...' her words were frozen as tears began to trickle down her eyes. And a nervous Silver was further dumbfounded in knowing what to do. Following his instincts, he grabbed hold of her and held her tight as she sobbed and welcomed the warmth from Silver.

'I am not what you think I am,' she began, 'And

I do not want to damage you...' Katya continued recounting her tale to Silver. How she had been sexually abused since the age of thirteen by her step-father. And that he still abused her, but she had managed to put up some resistance over the years. She spoke about how she hated her mother who knew of the abuse but instead was jealous of the attention and obsession the stepfather had for Katya. She then yelled in fury how she wished they both just died and fell into tears again.

'You different from other men, I like you, Silver. Sorry if I ruined your evening, I really wanted to thank you properly,' she said wiping her tears away and forcing a smile. Silver did not know what to do and simply caressed her hair down to her shoulder as he looked at her with a little pity and a smile. 'Katya, there is also more to me...' began Silver as he told her everything about him, how he was of the Slang Nyoka clan. Once he was done, he expected her to ran away, instead, she had listened to everything he had said, intrigued. She kissed him once he was done and then softly said, 'I guess we both damaged goods.'

Katya eventually slept on his chest as he looked up at the ceiling, gently stroking her hair. She left the next day, but she stayed on his mind. Silver laughed at himself in the mirror as he muttered, 'You in love.'

Katya came from a very wealthy family, her father had died unexpectedly from being poisoned, and Katya suspected her mother to have been behind it.

The father, Hector Hess, was involved in Feiville's highly competitive property development sector, which had ties with the underworld of crime. His business was beginning to fail, and a competitor was willing to buy him off, but Hector was not ready to give up yet. The competitor would become to be Katya Hess's stepfather, and his name was Anthony Soar. Katya believed her mother whose name was Emily, feared the family would lose their wealth and already experiencing trouble in her marriage, poisoned Hector and married Anthony, who would later buy out Hector's business as soon as he died. Hector's partners did not share his hard-headedness and yielded immediately.

Silver wondered if he could help Katya, maybe he could use his skills, kill Anthony and take her away but then he remembered his true aim was to amass five hundred duels. His martial way of life would probably not be fitting for Katya. His mind and heart battled it out, and his heart eventually won. He had already a hundred deadly duels to his name, it was time he took a break. Katya needed to be saved and he was the right person for the job he thought.

She invited him one evening, to one of the high-end restaurants of Feiville, where the two fine dined to the frowning stares of Feiville's wealthiest, who immediately recognised Katya. However, the two love birds giggled and smiled at each other not caring one bit. At the end of the evening, Silver assisted Katya in catching a taxi back home, and he instead decided to digest the evening further by taking a walk. He had never been so happy in his life and a smile permanently was painted on his face.

Hearing footsteps behind him his face suddenly changed, and a blank expression removed the prior smile and Silver kept walking, looking ahead he turned into an alley with one way out. Walking to the dead end, he stopped and then turned to stare at his followers, who had not tried to be discreet.

The three followers were three rough looking men, who looked like the typical hoodlums. Each one brandishing knives. 'Do not think I am the one that is trapped my friends,' said Silver as he slowly strolled towards them and then begin to hiss like a snake. The men in silence charged for him and within thirty seconds two out of the three were dead and the last one begged for his life as Silver grabbed him by the shirt, while he lay on the ground. 'Who sent you?' he asked glaring deep into the eyes of the man. 'I will tell you if you do not kill me,' answered the man fearfully. 'It does not make a difference. Silver placed his hand on the top of the man's head and within a sudden received all the information he needed. He caught a vision of the man who wanted him dead, it was Anthony Soar. Once he removed his hand from the top of the man's head, the man had died.

Katya upon returning to her home, a large mansion in the high mountain's that looked over

Feiville, where most of the old money of Feiville lived, was immediately summoned by Anthony. She ignored the order, but his henchmen who met her as the taxi dropped her off, grabbed her and forcefully dragged her to his study.

Dropping her inside, Anthony Soar nodded at his henchmen and they immediately left closing the door behind them. Katya was thrown on the ground landing on the study room's carpet, which was made of tiger skin. She got up as she was panting for air, breathing heavily, given that she was resisting going to the study.

Crossing her arms, she rebelliously looked at Anthony, who was dressed in a red bath robe with red slippers on. 'Embarrassing me again I see,' he said, looking at her with disgust. 'Like I give a shit,' responded Katya as she looked away. Seething in fury, Anthony who was a tall middle-aged man with balding hair, angrily marched towards her grabbing her by the hands and violently shook her before throwing her on the ground. He then quickly removed his bathrobe, he pounced on Katya while she was on the ground forcefully turning her, that her face was on the ground. He pulled up the dress she wore, while she screamed, 'NOOO!' Finally, once inside of her, he then begins to thrust and he murmured, 'You like this, don't you...you little bitch.'

In the morning, after showering while crying

Katya headed to the kitchen, her stepfather had left, and she was instead graced by the presence of her mother. She also had red hair like her daughter with an irresistible beauty, age had not withered this away. Except she was slightly paler and glanced at her daughter without hiding her hate. Katya responded in kind with a hateful glance.

'So, you spent the evening with him again,' grunted Emily, Katya's mother. Katya simply sighed and ignored her mother as she walked away. 'Do not walk away from me! You whore!' bellowed Emily as Katya left.

Silver had made up his mind, he was going to kill Anthony Soar and Emily Hess. Then he was going to leave Feiville with Katya. He did not know where they would go after that, but they will figure it out. He had not heard from her in days, and knowing Anthony had hired men to kill him, more was to come, so Silver kept a very low profile. Instead, he stalked Katya from afar, seeing how Anthony's men kept tabs on her. One day, he decided to reveal himself to her, after he had killed the men who followed her. Something she was not aware of herself, she was coming out of a boutique during the day and there outside stood Silver.

Joy filled her face as she smiled and then she asked teasingly, 'You have been following me hey?' Silver quickly responded honestly with, 'Yes.' He then quickly got serious telling her what had happened to him the evening after their dinner and that Anthony had men out to kill him. Katya did not mention her horrid ordeal after the dinner and simply her eyes got teary. With Silver gently holding her by the chin as he said, 'I will kill your stepfather and mother today. And then I want you to come with me.' They then hugged each other, and Katya's tears eventually trickled down.

That evening Silver got to work, using his skills he sneaked into the mansion, his first victim was Emily. She was busy removing her make up when he struck. She had caught a glimpse of his reflection in her mirror and as she opened her mouth to scream, no words came out except the sounds of her choking to death. Once he was done, he stealthily made his way to Anthony's study where Anthony was on a call. He sounded angry as he spoke to the person at the other end of the line, 'If the Sobek family think they can stop me from setting a foot in Wobbleton, they clearly do not know what I am made of!' Silver went inside opening the door immediately and then closed it behind him, as he turned to stare at Anthony, who looked bedazzled by Silver's presence. He knew who Silver was, his henchmen had taken photographs of Silver with Katya. Anthony simply could not believe that Silver had gone past the security. 'What do you want?' he asked with authority as he tried to project some form of composure. 'Nothing but your life,' Silver quickly answered as he stretched out his hand and formed a fist and as his fist got tighter, the quicker life slipped away from Anthony. As he choked helplessly, surprised by what was happening. He was gone after a minute and fell with a thud. The phone Anthony had used dangled from its chord with the speaker on the other end still on the call going, 'Hello? Hello!?' Silver simply hang the phone as he walked to Anthony's dead body.

Katya was by the Inn where Silver stayed, and smiling ear to ear, when she saw him enter the room. She quickly hugged him as he said, 'You will be safe from now on.' He did not have to say anymore, she could read from his eyes that he had done what he sought out to do.

She took a few steps back and by the time she was close to the bed, she opened her hands and jumped on the bed. Falling on her back and bounced back up slightly. Looking back at Silver seductively, she murmured, 'Fuck me.' Silver wasted no time as he walked towards her.

It was Silver's first-time making love that night and he enjoyed every moment of ravishing Katya. Once they were done, they shared a moment of just staring at each other, and then they both broke into a giggle. Both were swimming in bliss, not worried about tomorrow.

The next few days was mayhem, newspapers went on a frenzy with the breaking news publication of the death of one Feiville's great business magnate and property developers, Anthony Soar. They spoke about the death of Emily

Hess as well and some spoke of the "Hess Curse". It was all that could be heard on the radio, and the people of Feiville were found discussing and debating the matter.

This murder case fell on the lap of the unwilling Detective Dawson. Whose superiors put under pressure to resolve the matter as soon as possible.

He even questioned Katya, however, she had an alibi and was not in, in addition, she did not have the ability to execute the murders. What baffled Detective Dawson was that there were no fingerprints found anywhere on Anthony or Emily's body that could explain the murder. The forensic report from the autopsy indicated possible strangulation.

Silver was ready to leave Feiville, however, Katya had told him that they first had to take a break from each other, especially with the police investigating the matter. This made sense to Silver as it would be good if they were not seen together. However, his heart would long for her. Meanwhile, Detective Dawson started to interrogate the help that worked in the mansion, he stopped focusing on who was the murderer and delve rather deeper in the family dynamics. One of the domestic workers revealed that they had heard noises of what could have been Katya being raped by Anthony Soar. It was further revealed that she did not get along with Emily Hess, her mother. Nonetheless, Detective Dawson simply concluded that Katya was a rebellious child. When his mind focused back on the question of who could have killed Anthony and Emily? The detective wondered if it was a potential rival of Anthony who put a hit on his rival, he was aware of the seedy elements that could be found in the property development space. Before he could scrap the idea of interrogating the maids of the mansion, one more revelation from one of them had him intrigued. It appeared Anthony was once complaining about a boy that Katya was seeing. Something told Detective Dawson to look further into this.

He found witness accounts of Katya going out fine dining with a young man who had wolf-like eyes. The trail ended there, and the good detective was about to give up on the case. However, during a random conversation with a young upcoming detective at a bar frequented mostly by cops, the young detective mentioned the increase of deaths in the underground fighting scene. Then, Detective Dawson went on to brag about how he made a name for himself back in the days by shutting down those events. The young detective then mentioned that he had caught wind of a young man eighteen years of age, that was said to have a hundred duels under his belt, all finishing with his opponents dying. 'His described as having yellow wolf-like eyes...' the young detective kept on talking with Detective Dawson tentatively listening now to every word.

The young detective spoke about how those who organised those events were beginning to spill the beans of the events that they organised. They were openly letting the police in on their business in the hopes of getting rid of this new character in town. He was disturbing their betting schemes on the fight, and this Detective Dawson realised was probably because this person did not want to throw away fights. Worse of all is that in his killing spree of hundred opponents there was suddenly beginning to be a shortage of street fighters in Feiville. Something that was never heard of, a quick contemplation from Detective Dawson was that fighters were now scared to fight.

There was no name for this stranger, and the underworld had been unable to take him out, they had tried to their regret and never tried again. Once the young detective was done talking, Detective Dawson took a sip of his beer and then lit a cigarette in that moment of silence. He took another puff before he said, 'If gangsters are knocking on our door for help...because they're scared, I think we have a demon on our hands.' 'I am surprised the Slang Nyoka have not taken him out,' mentioned the young detective. And then Detective Dawson quickly replied, 'Those shadow dwellers are experiencing a civil war of some sort, amongst themselves...' cutting Detective Dawson, the young detective interrupted with disbelief on his face, 'What?!' 'Yes,' calmly began Detective Dawson, 'My friends in the Union of Nations have mentioned this...I cannot confirm and say it's true...but if it is, better those lot fight amongst themselves,' he concluded and took another puff. Then it came to him, 'Hold on!' he exclaimed as his cigarette nearly popped out his mouth, 'yellow eyes...this character most likely is from the Slang Nyoka. Probably a renegade.' The young detective frowned in disbelief and this annoyed Detective Dawson as he sighed to calm down, 'Look, kid, invite me when you guys are doing one of them raids...In fact it's an order!' he said pointing his finger and then he took another puff of his cigarette, crushed what remained on an ashtray and then gulped the remaining beer. Before burping loud and slamming the glass on the table and then he stormed out.

Silver felt heartbroken, something he did not understand. Katya had not broken up with him, although they did agree to be apart (an idea Katya had proposed) while the police investigated the murder of her mother and stepfather. She had not agreed nor said yes when he proposed that they leave after the scandal. Katya had simply smiled, and this to him was not enough. To clear his head, he decided he needed another duel. If they did not give him an opponent, whoever he set his eyes on that night will be his adversary.

He had received the usual eyes from the crowds, mostly that of fear and hate. With a couple of fans and few fake smiles of respect. Silver expected the organisers to be reluctant with him, in proposing a fight, nevertheless to his surprise, they invited him into one of their VIP booths, at the night club were some of the fights occurred. All smiling at him offering him drinks and all kinds of drugs which he bluntly denied. Something was up and he did not what it was, but if they tried to kill him like they once tried previously, they will pay dearly.

What really confused him, is that they even had a fighter for him, wasting no time and excited to see this fighter, Silver headed to the pit. His opponent was twice his size, muscular and a towering mountain, who was welcomed by Silver's smirk. His opponent did not look scared and stared at Silver like if he was the prey and before the clash could begin, the sounds of police sirens stopped the fight before it even began. Silver looked around in confusion, it was the first time he had experienced a raid. And thought it better to be calm cool and collected. On the other hand, his opponent, who Silver suspected must have been from out of town, fearlessly made his way his direction. Silver was nearly taken off guard and had suddenly turned back to his opponent. Before the man could seize him, he froze in his steps and Silver glared at him. The opponent grabbed his neck as he choked, confused and not knowing what was happening, while his breath slipped away within seconds and he was then dead.

'Put your fucking hands up!' bellowed a police officer from behind Silver, and he slowly turned around in response with no words, he simply stared at the cop and then placed his hands up. He noticed that the police officer was a bit shaky and nervous. And then came another figure, a man wearing a long turncoat and a hat, with a cigarette fuming with smoke. This man was Detective Dawson and to Silver's intrigue, he looked excited to see Silver. 'Arrest this kid, what are you waiting for! Come now I ain't got the whole day!' Detective Dawson snapped at the officer. 'Sir...you did not witness...what I.... j-us-t witnes-sed,' the police officer begins to shake uncontrollably. And it seemed Detective Dawson had an idea what the officer was referring to, 'Give me the handcuffs!' he barked and the police officer lowered his gun and then handed the handcuffs to Detective Dawson who then marched towards Silver who was forcefully handcuffed by the detective who added once he was done, 'I am old school kid! To hell with your rights! You may shut the fuck up! Or anything you do or say will be the cause of you missing and not showing up in court!'

Silver was calm and not bothered with the arrest, he was kept handcuffed in an interrogation room, seating down. There was a bright light bulb lighting up the centre of the table where he sat, and the rest of the room was dark. The light bulb dangled from the ceiling and Silver looked at the light, glancing at it now and then.

The door of the room opened, and Detective Dawson stepped in with a cup of coffee and a couple of files. He slammed the door behind, and strolled towards the opposite empty seat, he first placed the cup of coffee and the files of paper and then he pulled out the seat and sat down. He leaned back, took a sip of his coffee. And then grinned at Silver who blankly stared back.

'Slang Nyoka,' began Detective Dawson, 'Now you are already in trouble for the illegal underground fighting you have taken part in, and yes despite those fighters signing their lives away should they die, you will still serve time. A hundred duels all leading to death…wait…hundred and one!' pausing Detective Dawson excitedly clapped his hands and then continued, 'That is the current number ain't it? So how many years or what type of qi gong training made you gain such skills?' Before Silver could muster some words Detective Dawson interrupted him, 'I am not an idiot I know it took you most of your stupid life? How old are you?' this time he kept quiet waiting for Silver to respond. Silver remained silent a bit longer and Detective Dawson pulled his face with a frown indicating he was waiting for an answer. 'I am eighteen years old,' Silver eventually answered. 'Holy dragons of the Dao!' exclaimed Detective Dawson.

He chuckled and then opened his file of papers and seriousness sunk in, 'Kid, I am more interested in something else, here!' Detective Dawson threw a photo at him and the image was a black and white photo of Anthony Soar's corpse. Detective Dawson then threw another photo and that was the photo of the corpse of Emily Hess. He then leaned forward as he took a sip of his black coffee. Its heavy smell permeating the room. His eyes were fixed on Silver, while Silver's eyes were fixed on the photos, his heart began racing and the only reason was not that he was caught, but Katya. He did not want anything bad to happen to her.

'You fucked up kid, you murdered those two...' begin Detective Dawson and just as he was about to continue, Silver immediately interjected, 'I did it!' The detective's eyes widened slightly he did not believe he would receive such a quick confession. 'Well I guess we can wrap this up,' said Detective Dawson as he grabbed the two photos put it back in the files and then took another sip of the coffee. He then sighed scratching his forehead and then said, 'You not telling me the whole story, you and this girl Katya she warped you in, didn't she?' Silver kept quiet and his facial expression had resumed its blankness. 'This girl I believe lived hell, her stepfather most likely raped her and did all kind of horrid things to her...But she is a piece of work...' pausing Detective Dawson pulled out another photo from his pocket and threw it on the table. And Silver from a glance at the photo felt like he had a lump on his throat and his heart beat with a knot, like a small pain. The picture showed Katya kissing an older man. 'That's Gene Kissler, a powerful property developer and one of Anthony's Soar's rivals or former rivals. I am showing you this because you need to know the truth, when you doing time. Because this whore will not visit you while you rot away. She is inherited her family's wealth and this Anthony's wealth, but that is not enough, her next victim is this sucker here, Gene Kissler.' Sipping the last of his coffee, Detective Dawson got up and begin strolling around as he was drowned deep in thought ignoring the presence of Silver, who was in some form of shock.

'You remind me of myself kid, I was a rebel in my younger days…In fact, you seem more disciplined. I come from an ancient bloodline of dragon handlers. My family practised the Dragon Style, I never completed it, instead, I fought in the streets. It was prison or the army the judge gave me the choice. So, I joined when Eastland still had its military force and then after the service, I joined the police. I do not know why I am telling you this…But how does a warrior like you of an ancient clan fall so low?' Detective Dawson then looked at Silver who was shaking in disbelief.

Disgust and pain were painted on his face as he would glance and look away at the photo of Katya kissing Gene Kissler. The man looked like he was Anthony Soar's age, he wore sunglasses in the picture. And Silver imagined killing the man over and over. Tears looked like they were ready to burst out of his reddened eyes. He then began to hiss, and then he snapped as he broke free from his handcuffs, they fell off his hands. Silver grabbed the photo, looked at it and then put it in his pocket. Detective Dawson was calmly staring back, waiting for Silver to make his next move.

Silver began to glare at him, and Detective Dawson cleared his throat and then he gently held it. Then he shook his head. Closing his eyes, he sighed, relaxing his sternum and his eyes immediately shot back open and Silver fell backwards as if he was punched straight in the face. He went off his feet and fell on his back. He slowly got up and then looked at Detective Dawson flabbergasted.

'You a fool, after what I have just told you about me, you think your cheap tricks will work on me kid?!' Detective Dawson began chuckling as he gently shook his head. 'The six unifications my boy, the mind, the emotion, the energy and the pairing of the joints, all combined can make one invincible. Those are the ancient words find in the classical martial art commentaries. Besides my chi is not weak,' he added. Silver was not giving up and rushed for Detective Dawson who blocked a strike for his throat and countered with a punch, hitting Silver down on the face and his head rocked back and the detective seized the moment. He followed through with an uppercut and all Silver saw was black.

Waking up suddenly Silver found himself in the back of a van, his hands felt like they were carrying a ton and so did his feet. He had heavy handcuffs on his feet and hands, holding his hands and feet tightly. Silver simply smirked and before he could do something about it. The van he was in, which was moving began to tumble and roll, had it knocked something? He wondered as his body slammed around the back of the van. The turbulent motion stopped and the doors of the back of the van flung open. Silver could not make out who or what it was, however, this thing or person had incredible strength and easy pulled him out with his heavy handcuffs.

He got up and moved his head slightly side to side, 'I am sure you can free yourself from that!' snarled the person who had pulled him out of the van. Silver immediately recognised the voice, it was that of Medillo. His figure stood there, towering over Silver and glaring at the heavy handcuffs. Silver yelled as he struggled and then he began to focus, his yell turned into a loud hiss and the handcuffs, exploded into fragments. Medillo hit a few of them out of his way.

'Good!' barked Medillo and continued, 'You do not deserve the Serpent name nor blood, I should decapitate you where you stand! You left the war we wage against your uncle and you end up falling for a girl, so much for fighting five hundred duels!' Medillo ended by making a sneering sound as he crossed his arms, glaring at Silver who had kept his head down in shame.

'I do not know what to say...' before Silver could continue Medillo moved in and grabbed him suddenly by the throat, lifting him off the ground as he began to choke him. Silver grabbed Medillo hand as he struggled to breathe. Holding for dear life with both hands, twisting Medillo's hand in vain, he then let go and stared at Medillo who begin to feel his own breath fade away. He immediately let go of Silver who coughed as he moved a few metres away.

He massaged his throat and caught a glimpse of a glaring Medillo who had recovered. Silver straightened himself up and stared back blankly, reducing his heartbeat as he calmed down slowing his breathing. Medillo then could feel his breath slipping away again, he in return calmly closed his eyes, settling himself down. His mind focusing on the area centimetres below his navel and then all around his waist, leading his intent to the ground. All of this within seconds, his eyes then shot open and at that moment Silver's head had cocked back as if he had been punched. He stumbled back in disbelief as his eyes widened and quickly set his eyes back on Medillo who was briskly walking towards him.

'How were you able to deflect that' enquired Silver with a slight frown on his face, still drowning in disbelief. Medillo stopped with just a metre separating him from Silver, he gazed at Silver with a cocky smirk, before taking seconds to answer, 'Your internal practice or in Daoist's terms your neigong has always been exceptional and as for me...I am a master of the opposite the external practice. I have exceeded everyone in the clan in that department, building strong muscles. However, of course, I know the importance of internal practice. And after what you did to me in the forest, I have come up with a defence. You have relied too much on this trickery of yours, you have forgotten the basics. Oh, Silver, I have been watching you from the shadows and I will bet that Detective Dawson has even deflected that!' Silver chuckled once Medillo was done speaking, and Medillo snarled back irritated, 'What is so damn funny! You have disgraced your clan...your namesake...' pausing he sighed. 'Thank you, I did not need the help though,' said Silver. 'Whatever, I am done here, I know you think of your siblings as being dead to you. Nevertheless, those who stand against your uncle are fighting, there is chaos. But the clan is still alive,' done speaking Medillo, strolled away disappearing into the evening darkness as Silver gazed at him. Once he was out of sight, Silver looked at the van as it lay upside down on the road and did not bother to check if they were any survivors. It was a prison van and he must have been heading to prison while awaiting trial. He eventually walked away, also disappearing in the dark.

He kept a low profile in the small towns and villages kilometres away from Feiville, never staying in the same place for longer than a day. He eventually found refuge in the Dragons' Lair, training and stayed there for a month. However, the sentiments to confront Katya were too strong for him to ignore he needed to see her, while his emotions raged with confusion. Once the month had passed, Silver made up his mind and left the Dragons' Lair, heading back to Feiville. He knew Detective Dawson was out there ready to send him to prison. Silver had made the police's most wanted list, and his name and face were on every newspaper.

Silver had painfully discovered that Katya had married Gene Kissler, and the couple lived in the hills far from the city where most of Feiville's old money resided. He had not seen her for about two months, and was yearning to confront her, like an addict seeking his fix.

Detective Dawson had a hunch Silver would return and despite the pressure, he had experienced from his superiors for Silver's escape, he remained calm. He was retiring soon from the police force and had already an excellent record that is why he was the top cop assigned to the task of capturing Silver. Detective Dawson, had an army of police officers not far from the mansion where Katya and Gene stayed, secretly watching them, waiting for Silver to appear. The couple were completely unaware, but Gene had his own security, being a property developer in Feiville and a man of status, he had a handful of hired guards patrolling his mansion.

The detective expected Silver to appear during the evening, the common assumption of when an assassin would make a move, especially one from the Slang Nyoka. But Detective Dawson was not aware that Silver had no intention of assassinating anyone and being one of the Slang Nyoka's most elite, he would not be so predictable. He was going to show up during the day, instead of the evening. Silver had scouted the area and was aware of the police's secret presence. More than that, what the detective was not aware of was Silver's level of stealth.

Silver sneaked into the mansion past the guards, a shadow stuck to the wall, he revealed himself in the bedroom Katya shared with her husband, Gene Kissler. She was busy seating, while she gently rubbed her face with cotton wool while looking at her reflection in the mirror.

Silver was taken aback by her beauty, he stared at her from the shadows for a few seconds and then revealed himself. Katya froze, her eyes widened, and she then swallowed anxiously staring at Silver's reflection from the mirror. She then slowly stood up and turned to look at Silver.

Their eyes met and she then looked down for a moment before looking back at him. 'You fucking betrayed me...you whore! So you used me to kill your parents and then you married this rich guy,' Silver had paused barely able to control his fuming fury as he looked around the room and then back at Katya, 'woman you broke everything inside...' drowning in silence again as he placed his right hand on his chest more to the left, the heartbreak was stronger in her presence. 'Silver...I don't know what to say...' Katya stopped speaking as she strolled towards Silver and her words run out. She then stood centimetres away from him smiling wryly as her eyes got wet. Silver sighed and tried to establish some calm within himself. Then he felt something, he scanned Katya looking down at her abdomen, and the sensation felt stronger. The stronger the feeling got the more he understood and then he knew what it was he sensed from Katya, she was pregnant.

He took a few steps back and grabbed his forehead while Katya frowned at him. Silver then noticed she seemed to have gained a bit of weight. The baby was his, he could feel the connection, there was a Slang Nyoka baby developing in that womb.

'You pregnant,' muttered Silver more confused than before, his negatives emotions were mixed with surprise and some feelings of joy. Sensing the energy emitting from Katya, Silver knew the baby was a boy. He walked towards her, placing his hands on her abdomen. 'It's my baby,' he said, placing his head against her abdomen as he knelt. 'Yes,' Katya muttered as her tears eventually began to trickle down and Silver got up to look at her straight in her eyes. He wiped away the tears, and then he heard foot steps heading to the room.

'Honey! Honey!' it was the voice of Gene Kissler and before Silver could even cloak himself into the shadows the door to the room flung open. Gene Kissler stepped in horror-stricken, he drew out his gun and began yelling, 'GUARDS! GUARDS! GET

AWAY FROM HER!' he pointed his gun, Silver glanced at it and then began to hiss, sensing the fear in Gene as he stood there pointing the gun and shaking uncontrollably. 'Gene...' Katya's words were halted as Gene interrupted immediately, 'It's OK honey, I will save you.' Silver continued hissing like a snake as he took a step, Gene began pulling the trigger firing multiple rounds. 'Nooo!' yelled Katya as she stepped in front of Silver who then pushed her out of the way, shocked by her act. He glared at Gene and then they both looked at Katya as she got up. The bullets had pierced her body and the blood had begun to leak out. She looked at Silver and muttered, 'I am sorry.' Katya then fell and Silver rushed to her side, he could feel her life and that of his unborn son fading away in seconds. Her eyes were looking at him and then they slowly closed, till he could finally feel she had died. Silver turned to Gene who could not believe what he had just done. Then he spotted the glare of Silver, 'You bastard!' grunted Silver igniting his rage as his hand stretched out and closed into a fist. At that moment Gene dropped his gun and held his neck choking in desperation. He began floating in the air and then the moment his lost breath passed he dropped dead on the ground hitting it with a thud, and Silver found himself in tears and slightly panting. Everything was rising as he hyperventilated struggling to breathe and then he sighed grabbing hold of himself, he sighed one more time closing his eyes, settling everything back down. He opened his eyes again, and peered around him and the nightmare was still there, however, he had now accepted it.

Silver noticed and felt that some of the fired bullets had only grazed his arm and shoulder, not penetrating his body in any way.

Sounds of police sirens could be heard approaching and footsteps rushing to the room. It was the handful of guards that guarded the mansion heading to the room. Silver immediately immersed into the shadows vanishing. Outside, the police got out of their cars, and heading the charge was Detective Dawson. They were completely caught off guard as the planning had been specifically only if Silver showed up during the night.

The police due to the investigation would pick up that Silver was not responsible for Katya's death. However, he was charged for the death of Gene Kissler. Katya and his unborn child would be something he always had on his mind and pain he would never forget.

CHAPTER THREE- MASTER OF THE TIGERS

Detective Dawson had retired without the capture of Silver who had made the list of the world's top most wanted men. His superiors held no weight in judging him of incompetence and although Silver was the first of his clan to be in the visible eye by name and face. He still upheld their reputation as he had escaped the police forces capture. Now he was in the eyes of the different police forces around the world and the Union of Nations.

He spent a few years simply training in solitude in different isolated places, choosing the forests and the mountains, his sole aim now was in accomplishing his life goal of five hundred duels. He would only appear from his hiding when he duelled and from his hundred duels, his numbers increased steadily over the years. His training became more intense and so did his focus. He duelled brawlers and martial artist masters reaching the number four hundred and ninety-eight by the time that he was thirty years of age. He had only two more duels left and by this time he was the most wanted man in the world.

Silver found refuge in Eastland's second biggest city Yu Town. It was another metropolis, bustling and busy like Feiville without the same underbelly and illegal activity.

He would disguise himself in public and had settled there only for a few months. His next opponent was a tiger master he was seeking. This master was the master of the Tiger Claw. It's not that he was known as the best around the world, but masters in the martial art community knew of this master as the best amongst all tiger styles practitioners. And when Silver defeated his last opponent a Crane master, he mentioned in his last dying breath the name of the master of tigers. All he told Silver in his dying moment was that the master of tigers lived in Yu town and that he was a butcher. Besides Silver knowing that the master lived in Yu Town, the other information that the master was a butcher did not really help. As Silver was to find out, a big city like Yu Town had a variety of butchers, nevertheless, he was not going to give up so easily. He wondered the city, disguised enjoying the scenery.

The thought of finding the tiger master had floated to the back of Silver's mind as he wandered through the city. During sunset, he headed to a bar downtown, and ordered a five-hundred-millimetre glass of beer, peacefully drinking.

His disguise was a hat and fake greying beard with a grey wig, however, his distinct yellow wolf-like eyes could not be hidden. The patrons of the bar did not bother with him and kept to themselves. Silver new Yu Town was different from Feiville, it did not have the same underground fighting scene and was more peaceful in that sense. However, as he sipped his beer, feeling the beginning sensations of tipsiness settle in, he gazed to his left and then felt his heart pump up his throat he nearly choked. A beautiful lady with red hair had caught his eyes, this woman looked like she was in her early twenties. Her greenish-brown eyes reminded Silver of Katya and he stood frozen staring at her while his beer got warm. She noticed he was staring, and Silver beamed at her, but she looked away nervously trying not to frown. Silver simply chuckled at this reaction and continued to drink peacefully.

Three rugged looking men entered the bar, they had caught Silver's attention as he looked at them from the corner of his eye, what intrigued Silver immediately was their bandaged hands. One them formed a fist as they moved their wrist and Silver knew they, martial artists. The man who was warming up his wrist started to make hand manoeuvres resembling a tiger's claw and then he would then form a fist as he did this. Silver did not need further confirmation the three men were martial artists.

His beer was finished and when he stood up, could feel he was a bit tipsy, with his legs feeling a bit weak. He strolled towards the three men and asked, 'Could you gentlemen tell me which school you from?' All three looked at each other before answering that question and then one of them answered, 'We do not practice martial arts.' Once he answered they all turned to each other with one turning to the bar ready to order the drinks. The other two then began speaking to each other ignoring Silver who then said more sternly, 'I have not asked about martial arts, just what school? I think...' Silver's words were stopped as one of the men glared back at him and walked closer towards him and said, 'Listen here, we do not care what you asked. I think it would be safe if you left us alone.' Silver smiled in response and walked away, leaving the bar.

Those three men were novices and even though he could kill them with a snap of a finger. He did not need to draw any unnecessary attention. The night had covered the skies and the roads were lit by the street lamp. A hooded towering figure had appeared in front waiting for Silver it seemed. He immediately revealed himself and Silver stopped just a metre in front of him and said, 'Medillo Serr.'

'How are your old friend?' asked Medillo. 'Cannot

complain, and you are still alive...my uncle still in charge?' responded Silver. 'He is not dead yet...there is more turmoil than before...it's a civil war and you should join us!' said Medillo, his eyes glaring at Silver who was not fazed. 'We both know that is not going to happen,' he replied to Medillo in disgust. Medillo sighed and then beamed at his old friend. 'What?' a bemused Silver asked. 'I have a son, my firstborn... his name is Medil,' answered Medillo. 'Good for you,' said Silver forcing a smile as the news reminded him of Katya and the wound still raw inside pained. 'So what? You still keeping tabs on me?' he asked changing the subject and Medillo responded, 'Yes, I have, since you not far from your goal of five hundred duels, I will give you a hint where the master of tigers is. He is a butcher The Clawing Tiger Butchery is the name of the place. He does not have a school, however, he does teach his employees. Anyway, I have a feeling this is the last time you will see me again.' With those last words, Medillo disappeared in the night.

Silver did not waste time and the following day he headed to the butchery. It was in the downtown area of Yu Town and the butcher specialised in hunted venison meat, he did deal with a variety of other meats. But hunting venison was the focus and when Silver had walked in there requesting a piece of venison steak. The butcher an old man with narrow eyes with epicanthic folds, ripped a slice off the hanging dead animal with his hands. Seizing and ripping with ease like a tiger on its prey. Despite the old man face showing ageing, the rest of his body was built like any young athlete of twenty-year-old. He was short and muscular, with big thick forearms. Silver knew that this was the master, he smiled as he packaged the meat and then gave it to Silver who beamed back. Once the meat was in his hands Silver threw it away and at the same time, he removed his disguise, not wanting to waste in more time.

'Do we have a problem?' the puzzled butcher asked. 'Not at all, Master Liang Claw,' said Silver citing the butcher's name. The butcher paused for a moment assessing Silver, he then forced a smile and turned his back to Silver. 'I am Silver Serpent,' began Silver as he removed more than his disguise; he was undressed till he was half naked. 'You want to taste the Claw family's tiger claw?' enquired Liang calmly gazing back at Silver. Silver beamed in response, 'Let's make this quick, I am so close to having five hundred deadly duels.' Liang snorted and sneeringly looked at Silver who had begun to hiss as his eyes slightly gouged out looking at Liang. He was slowly stepping towards Liang, like a slow slithering snake. Liang quickly removed his bloodied butcher apron, throwing it on the ground and then he barked, 'Do you think that hissing scares me!'

The butchery had some staff members on the day, and Liang gestured for them not get involved and all they did was watch with their eyes wide. Liang grabbed hold of a cleaver and threw it directly at Silver, who immediately dodged it. The cleaver got stuck to the wall, and Silver quickly glanced at it, before looking at Liang who glared back. Silver beamed at the attack and waited to see what else Liang had, 'What is going through your mind old man,' he teased, and a sneering smirk brushed itself on his face.

The master of tigers went straight for Silver, striking him with a series of punches. Silver deflected a couple before receiving one straight punch on the nose, his head rocked back as he stumbled. He shook his head and when he looked straight Liang had just launched a roundhouse kick, which Silver dodged by ducking underneath. He then grabbed hold of Liang's one leg and lifted him up, slamming him straight hard into the ground. He knelt for the final blow and with his hands shaped like the head of a snake, Silver immediately struck Liang straight between the eyebrows and Liang within two seconds had his head slightly back with his chin raised. Silver closed his eyes and the master of tigers was dead.

Silver stood up and said, 'His dead,' as he panted slightly for air, with those last words he walked out of the butchery as the eyes set on him, looked at him fearfully. Once he had left, the staff immediately rushed for Liang's corpse.

CHAPTER FOUR- COLE SUD

Easex was the capital city of the East-South Union, not quite bustling like the metropolis of Feiville. However, like most big cities it had its share of skyscrapers. With plenty of ancient cites, which were always flocked by tourists and the pigeons they fed.

It was also home for the main branch of the Sud family, a very ancient clan, renowned for they Sud Fist, the family's martial art. And practising in the courtyard of the family villa was Cole Sud. A tall black man in his twenties, he had a small goatee and thick eyebrows with no hair but complete baldness.

His face remained serene and devoid of emotion as he moved in the courtyard slowly. Practising the Sud Fist and trying to remain in constant speed and acceleration. Whether he changed directions from left to right, front to back, he remained constant in pace. Movements that tried to achieve stillness. He had been moving for hours and the sweat was dense and not dripping.

'Brother!' shouted a voice as Cole Sud finished his movements returning to his beginning position and remaining there as calmed everything down. He then slowly turned after a moment towards where the voice had come from and caught a glimpse of a tall black man about his height, also bald but with a thick beard and the family trait of having thick eyebrows. It was his older brother Ren Sud. 'Yes, what do you want?' asked Cole. Ren Sud said nothing and instead threw a rolled-up newspaper he held in his hands. Cole caught it and his brother said in a commanding tone, 'Read it!' he then hurriedly walked away.

Cole Sud unrolled the newspaper and headed to the front page and the article title read, "Phoenix Guan Former Lei Tai Champion Criticizes the Sud Fist" Cole chuckled and simply threw the newspaper away. His brother was teasing him and wanted him to part take in the Lei Tai, a martial art tournament that took place once a year, were the world's elite martial arts duelled each other, sometimes to the death.

'The Sud Fist does not need the Lei Tai,' he muttered to himself. After his morning training, he headed to town during the afternoon, the sun was blazing, and Cole simply needed to relax.

He ended relaxing in a park bench while gazing a people picnicking and dogs chasing whatever their owners threw at them. The peace made him inhale and then exhale. The ambience was as peaceful for him as anything could get.

Turning his head, he saw a young adolescent male sprinting away while being chased by two men dressed in uniform. Cole recognised the uniform, it was that of Union Troops and not the police. Cole hated the fact that Union Guards were also doing the policing in Easex. All eight nations of the world had stopped having their own armies and the Union of Nations instead had taken the role. But the job should have been maintained but each nation's police force. Watching those Union Guards made Cole Sud rage with anger, they had eventually caught up with the adolescent as one of them tackled him to the ground. They soon handcuffed him and lifted him off the ground while he helplessly yelled and screamed. One of the Union Guards, then hit the adolescent on the back of his head knocking him out instantly.

The whole commotion had destroyed the peace Cole experienced, his eyes were locked in on the whole situation. As he fought his mind to do anything about it, but before he knew it, he had stood up and started walking the direction of the Union Guards, who had begun radioing for back up. Cole's slow stroll immediately morphed into him marching towards the Union Guards.

'Hey! Hey! Guys just a citizen's curiosity...what has he done?' frowning and trying to mask his contempt, Cole waited for an answer from the

Union Guards. 'Listen here, it would be better if you worried about your own business!' snarled the one Union Guard. The other stood silent glaring at Cole.

Their response made Cole stand his ground and still controlling the boiling blood that coursed his veins he said, 'It's my right as a citizen to know, besides you two are just soldiers what do you know about policing?' The two Union Guards glanced at each other first as a response and then the one responded with more aggression, 'This mutt! Was throwing zap signs. We then had to teach him a listen! Now FUCK OFF!'

Cole had seen red, and he stood there silent not glaring his temper had flowed up and back down as he gently sighed. His sternum slightly went in and he felt a drop just below the navel, while his upper back lifted slightly and was rounded. His shoulder slightly moved forward and the joints in knees were slightly bent.

'We might have to arrest you as well!' snapped the other Union Guard. 'I am not going anywhere,' said Cole blankly as he stared at the Union Guards. One of them looked away for a split second as Cole broke his mental armour. 'Here hold him,' said the one Union Guard who held the now unconscious adolescent and passed him to the other Union Guard. He then slowly walked towards Cole while maintaining an intimidating glare. By the time he was about an arm's length away and tried to move to attack Cole, as his mind communicated the movement and his body attempted it, Cole was already on him. All he did was strike the Union Guard in his throat. Choking and mildly coughing, the Union Guard held his throat as he lowered his body a bit. The other guard holding on to the adolescent threw the adolescent to the ground. And the young man remained unconscious as he hit the grass of the park. 'You bastard!' he exclaimed and drew out his gun pointing it straight at Cole. 'Shoot! I dare you!' Cole fearlessly taunted the Union Guard realising that it was madness, however, there was no turning back now.

'Come! Shoot me! In public! The people of Easex do not want you guys here!' Cole started raising his voice drawing more attention as people stared on at the ongoing events. 'Fuck off!' screamed an old man amongst the gathering crowd, and he was joined by others. The Union Guard pointing the gun seemed to be getting nervous and radioed once more for the backup anxiously as he put away his gun. Cole moved in and with the help of others around him, they grabbed hold of the unconscious adolescent. Placing his hand on the adolescent's shoulders, Cole resuscitated the young man within seconds, as the adolescent eyes slowly opened.

Back up had arrived for the Union Guards, flash bangs and tear gas were used to clear the area. Cole and those who helped had managed to carry the young man during the commotion that occurred.

FIVE HUNDRED DEADLY DUELS

The two Union Guards were saved by their back up and the event was the front page the next day. Neither Cole or the adolescent were arrested, however, the event had erupted protest and debate in the streets of Easex. Within weeks, Union Guards no longer patrolled the streets and the Easex police were the only ones allowed to police, however, this was for now. The situation had changed Cole forever and he had become highly suspicious of the Union of Nations. An entity he had become to see as increasingly oppressive.

The news of the events in Easex circulated the world and could be heard in the soundwaves. Silver was in a bar gazing at the black and white image of the reporter, reporting on the events that occurred at Easex. He was having a glass of water in his disguise and the barman who was wiping a piece of glass clean glanced at the TV, which had begun to struggle to display the report. 'Damn television, I hate this new technology. It's not even in colour!' he said and hit the TV and it switched off, further frustrated he walked to the radio and switched it on, 'There! Better!' he added.

Silver remained silent and once he was done drinking his water, he walked out. Walking down the streets, he pondered of his next duel. He was now on four hundred ninety-nine, just one more left. A smile brushed itself on his face and then it disappeared, in the beginning achieving the goal was exciting, he could confirm that he was a brilliant martial artist, but the hole, if he was the world's best, could not be closed. A reality that had dawned on him through his duels. Nonetheless, he had to see it to the end.

CHAPTER FIVE- THE KING OF BRAWLERS

Somewhere in the vast mountainous area that was the Dragon's Lair, was an old man, with a complete grey beard and long hair stopping by his shoulders. Wild like his habitat, the man was at peace in his loneliness. Dressed in rugs and meditating in a sitting position, while listening to the downstream of the mountain river. This man was Detective Dawson, now retired, he had to most people's surprise, favoured life in the mountains like the ancient Daoist hermits who once dwelled in the area.

Despite the complete greying of his hair, the former detective had regained a vitality he had lost during his policing years. He had the muscle mass of any young man and if not more energy. He had stopped smoking and drinking black coffee. Instead, he had begun drinking the green tea leaves that grew in the area.

Having not completed his Dragon Style training, he had at least mastered its eight known palms, which were fundamentals to the style. And in his years in the army, he was introduced to the Harmonious Fist, a martial art from the Sol Islands. It was taught by one of its best practitioners Kazak Subek and Detective Dawson became his best student. He would include the concept of the six harmonies or unification in his practice of the eight palms of the dragon style.

The six harmonies which were a concept found in all martial arts but greatly emphasised in the Harmonious Fist was the idea of uniting the three external pairs and three internal pairs. The three external pairs, referred to the pairing of the hips to the shoulders, the knees to the elbows and the feet to the hands. The three internals referred to the pairing of the mind with the emotions, the mind with the energy and the energy (or as the Daoist would say qi pronounced ch'i) with the body.

'So, this is what has happened to the great Detective Dawson,' commented a voice and Detective Dawson slowly opened his eyes. Still sitting in his meditation posture, he gazed at the person who had spoken and then begins warming down from his meditation. The person simply looked till Detective Dawson was done. Now standing up Detective Dawson said, 'Drasul… you found me.' 'Yes, grand uncle I have, so why our ancestral home, you hoping to complete your training?' Detective Dawson sighed and then said,

'What I know is enough, I may not have the power of the last flame like you do, but it's not like it would have made the training any easier.'

Drasul Stockhorn was Detective Dawson's grandnephew. The detective was the older brother of Drasul's grandfather and the uncle to Drasul's father. Detective Dawson's original name was Dragonson Stockhorn. The Dragonson was then changed to Dawson Stockhorn, from him joining Eastland's army when the country had its own military. He had joined an elite special forces unit that had a tradition of changing names, and he had kept the Dawson name.

'So how has the Union been treating you?' asked Detective Dawson as he looked into his nephew's piercing sky blue eyes. 'I am done with the Union of Guards, I am now opening shop as a bounty hunter,' answered Drasul. 'Not joining the police force?' asked Detective Dawson. 'Not for me, besides I want to catch Silver Serpent,' said Drasul confidently. 'There is no need for that Drasul,' begin Detective Dawson and Drasul slightly frowned as he listened attentively, 'Silver Serpent will be on the lookout for me, I will be his five hundredth duel.' 'Why you say that?' asked a puzzled Drasul as Detective Dawson finished. 'Feiville has historically housed the best fighter or brawlers. It is where the best in the world historically flocked to challenge the best, long before the formation of the Union of Nations and the staging of one big Lei Tai tournament,' answered

Detective Dawson. 'Talk about the Lei Tai, why did he not just part take in that tournament?' a frowned Drasul asked. 'The Lei Tai is a farce in deciding the quality of the martial artist. I was the best of Feiville, his bound to find that out or he probably already knows. He could not challenge me then because he was not of standard,' said Drasul. 'So, you do not want me to catch him because you want to fight him?' Drasul's frown had increased as he gazed at the detective as if he was a mad man. The detective beamed back at his nephew and sniggered before saying, 'My master Kazak Subek has demanded my presence in the Sol Islands, I suggest you come as well. Before you ask, he wants to meet with me to discuss serious matters, the discussion will be around the Union of Nations. Frederick Sobek will be there I believe, your friend from the Union Guard.' 'Yes he did mention he will be visiting his ancestral home,' said Drasul holding his chin as he pondered and then he added, 'Yes and back on the subject of Silver...' the detective drowned his words as he interrupted him with, 'forget that, Silver will show up, you might be powerful but Silver is of the Slang Nyoka clan, he can hide in the shadows better than any of us.'

Drasul and Detective Dawson had travelled a month later by plane to the Sol Islands, landing in the Islands' newly launched international and only airport. A few days after their landing, in the evening under the starless sky with a full moon, was

FIVE HUNDRED DEADLY DUELS

a small fishing vessel approaching the Solese shore. A hooded figure hoped out of the boat, leaving the decaying bodies of the owners of the boat as he strolled on the wet sands of the shore.

The next day, emergency sirens could be heard from the main island and the other nearby islands. The group of militiamen and women responsible for the policing and protection of the island had come across the murder and the shipping boat. The victims had died by strangulation, however, there were no external physical signs of strangulation. Nonetheless, proceedings were happening at the Council of Masters' chamber, which was housed in an ancient temple. Inside the chamber were benches where the masters sat, that surrounded a large painting in the centre of the chamber, of two fishes of different colours that were facing different directions. This painting symbolised the yin yang symbol, and on the ceiling of the chamber was a painting. It displayed Felix Subek the First, leading his men into a naval battle. He was the one who had unified the different clans in the Sol Islands and was the founder of the Council of Masters.

Detective Dawson and Drasul stood in the centre of the chamber while being gazed by the masters. The doors to the chambers were opened and a militiaman in uniform entered to announce what had been see by the shore close to the beach. The man they reported to nodded calmly before barking out, 'Sort it out!' and the militiaman nodded back and hurriedly left closing the chamber door.

The man who had barked out the order had thick eye brows, hazel eyes with epicanthic folds and a long black beard that was beginning to grey. He was completely bold and had serious tense facial expression, this man was Kek Subek, the leader of the chamber, holding the title Chairman Master.

'Let's carry on with the proceedings, we will sort out that matter once we are done here,' said a man seating not far from Kek. This was Detective Dawson's master, Kazak Subek and Kek Subek's son. Bald like his father and sharing the same intense serious facial expression. They looked like twins, however, Kazak was beardless and tall.

'Dragonson Stockhorn and Drasul Stockhorn,' began Kek Subek as his voice was transmitted throughout the chamber due to its excellent acoustics, 'we glad to have you two here, getting to the point. The Union of Nations have been sending an armada of ships to surround the islands, their pathetic excuse is for our protection,' a smile briefly appeared on both Kek and Kazak's face and then disappeared as it came and Kek continued, 'but we, not fools! We have made our preparations, we need to monitor and start a secret resistance against the Union of Nations. It started off in Feiville, Eastland and you two are from there we need you two to be our eyes and ears. Like my grandnephew,' Kek pointed at the young man that was black and with similar thick eyebrows and serious facial expression. And this grandnephew was Frederick Sobek, 'he has passed us this information, and we expecting the Union to tell us about this sometime. Good thing we already know...' Kek abruptly stopped, something had caught his eyes in the shadows of the chamber. The shadow moved then immediately revealed was a hooded figure. His appearance immediately made Kek and Kazak rise from their seat. The hooded person appeared behind Detective Dawson and Drasul. It removed its hood, and the person was Silver Serpent who with a murderous smirk looked at Detective Dawson who simply blankly stared at him. Drasul knew Silver's face and could not hide his surprise as his eyes slightly widened at Silver. He now understood what his grand-uncle meant when he mentioned Silver's ability to hide in the shadows.

Silver wasted no time and he leapt for Detective Dawson with a punch, the detective evasively moved out of the way. And Silver turned to launch his next attack but was pushed back by a sharp sidekick from the detective with the edge of his foot towards Silver's liver. He winced a bit in pain showing this for a split second before he bounced back for his third attack. But the lightning spark of current from the hands of Kek, zapped him from behind and Silver yelled in pain and then gritted his teeth trying to resist and then he fell to his knees. Kek withdrew his hand which he had outstretched.

Silver then struggled to get up but managed to get to his feet panting, he wiped the sweat from his forehead as he cast a glare at Kek. 'You probably the first Slang Nyoka or even the first person to breach this sacred chamber,' began Kek calm as he spoke. 'Any snakelets in training back at the clan, can infiltrate this place, no offence,' responded Silver calming down and recharging his zapped-out energy. 'Silver Serpent let me not beat around the bush, we expected your presence, Dragonson told us you might show up, the dead fishermen by the shore, clearly your doing. So, you clearly were hearing our conversation regarding the Union of Nations?' once done Kek waited for Silver's response. 'I heard everything, but I am a warrior and I only care of...' Silver's words were halted by Detective Dawson's words, 'You only care about your five hundred duels? You a warrior? Well, we have a potential war in our hands, like that of ancient time, when the Southern States and the Sol Islands fought against General Fei. Being a cop in Feiville, I have seen corruption from the bottom and the top, we want you to join us, Silver.'

Drasul was shocked by these words, and with widened eyes and a bemused facial expression, he frowningly gazed at Detective Dawson. 'Yes, join us!' exclaimed Kazak and Frederick Sobek also stood from his seat repeating the same, 'Join us.' Silver looked around the chamber at all the masters, for a moment he felt overwhelmed and then closed his eyes sighed and then re-opened them, he was now calm and settled.

'My sole goal in this life is to fight five hundred duels, now I just want to complete what I started,' said Silver as he looked around and stopped at Detective Dawson. 'If we give you your five hundredth duel would you then join us?' asked Detective Dawson. 'Yes, I guess I won't have a choice,' Silver rapidly responded as he cast a glance at Kek and Kazak. 'Fine!' exclaimed Detective Dawson, 'Clear me some space and Drasul this is the ancient way of duelling...do not avenge me. Whatever happens, let it be!' he added and Drasul simply nodded and cleared away by giving the detective and Silver some space for the duel.

They both greeted each other with the yin-yang sign, the left-hand open, while the right hand was closed in a fist. Then the fight began, Silver rushed forth stepping as he lowered his body slightly. His feet stance would switch simultaneously with the hands positioned like the head of a snake as he hissed. He then struck out, and the detective evasively escaped it as he stepped out and around in a circular motion and then countered with a roundhouse kick that knocked Silver a few steps back. Excited Detective Dawson pounced to finish Silver off. But Silver Serpent quickly got up feeling hazy as the detective threw a straight vertical punch, that Silver deflected with one hand and then struck the detective underneath in the armpit area.

Detective Dawson froze his eyes widened and then Silver gave him front kick on the chest knocking him down. The detective struggled to get up as blood dripped out of his nose. 'The serpent strikes with venom!' exclaimed Silver and then he greeted detective with the yin-yang gesture. Detective Dawson cast a glance at Drasul who nodded and then beamed at his grand uncle who also responded likewise before falling again. He shook violently for a few seconds and then stopped, he was dead.

'Five hundred deadly duels, I realised a while back that reaching the number would not make me the strongest, but I had set out to do it, and therefore I needed to finish it. It is the way of the Slang Nyoka to finish a kill or die doing your best to achieve it. I will join your cause,' with those last words Silver's body drowned down to the floor appearing like a shadow that moved quickly and out through the doors of the chamber.

Months later Silver handed himself to the police in the city of Wobbleton, he was sent to Main Central, the Sud-Republic's most dangerous prison, where it housed the worse of the worse. Upon his arrival, he was kept in a room seated, while his hands and feet were handcuffed. The warden wanted to meet him, and he sat patiently waiting in the dim lit room. The warden walked in with two heavily guarded guards. She was a beautiful woman with short blonde hair and green eyes. Her face was riddled with seriousness and a no messing around facial expression. She sat and piercingly looked at Silver with no fear and he beamed back. The armed guards stood by her side, standing up.

'Right, I have read your file and I wanted to be brief for today, if I had my way, putting you to death would save us a lot of trouble...' the warden stopped speaking, as Silver began to chuckle. 'Excuse me, what's fucking funny?' she glared at him and Silver's chuckle turned to nothing but a murderous smirk, and the guards who stood beside the warden, dropped their weapons and within a second, both dropped dead. 'Listen here you bitch, since you know a great deal about me, you would know that I handed myself in and in any moments time I can leave should I wish to, now please, take me to my cell,' said Silver as the warden shook in shock. 'Call the goddam guards!' barked Silver, and the warden shook even more frighteningly as she winced with tears of terror trickling down her eyes.

He was later taken to his cell by fearful armed guards, sentenced to life in prison. Silver would receive daily visits from Frederick Sobek, about the movement in play to resist the Union of Nations' potential threat to the world.

THE END